To Sophie, Brian, Eddie, and Johnny.

Library of Congress Cataloging-in-Publication Data:

Names: Ruzzier, Sergio, 1966- author, illustrator.
Title: The quiet boat ride and other stories / by Sergio Ruzzier.
Description: San Francisco, California : Chronicle Books LLC, [2019] |
Series: Fox + Chick ; book 2 | Summary: Fox enjoys quiet boat rides
and watching the sunrise, but Chick is noisy and hyperactive
and frequently disrupts their adventures—nevertheless
they remain friends and enjoy their time together.
Identifiers: LCCN 201800942 | ISBN 9781452152899 (alk. paper)
Subjects: LCSH: Foxes—Juvenile fiction. | Chicks—Juvenile fiction. | Friendship—
Juvenile fiction. | Patience—Juvenile fiction. | Humorous stories. | CYAC: Foxes—Fiction. |
Chickens—Fiction. | Friendship—Fiction. | Patience—Fiction. | Humorous stories. |
LCGFT: Humorous fiction.
Classification: LCC PZ7.R9475 Qu 2019 | DDC [E]—dc23
LC record available at https://lccn.loc.gov/2018009424

Manufactured in China.

Design by Sara Gillingham Studio.
Handlettering by Sergio Ruzzier.
The illustrations in this book were rendered in pen, ink, and watercolor.

10 9 8 7 6 5 4 3 2

Chronicle Books LLC
680 Second Street
San Francisco, California 94107
www.chroniclekids.com

SERGIO RUZZIER'S
FOX + CHICK

THE QUIET BOAT RIDE

and Other Stories

chronicle books · san francisco

CONTENTS

THE QUIET BOAT RIDE

WHAT ARE YOU DOING, FOX?

I'm going for a quiet boat ride.

6

CHOCOLATE CAKE

26

THE
SUNRISE

May I come
with you?

Okay, but hurry!
I don't want
to miss it.

No problem.
I'll be right down.

What should I wear, Fox?

Chick, please hurry.

Should I take
an umbrella?

It's not
raining, and
if it was, we
wouldn't see
any sunrise.

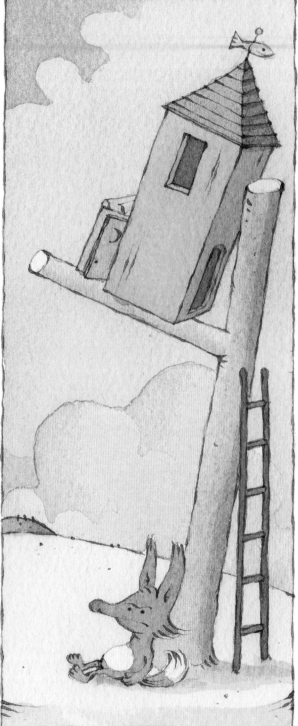

37

Where's this sunrise, Fox?